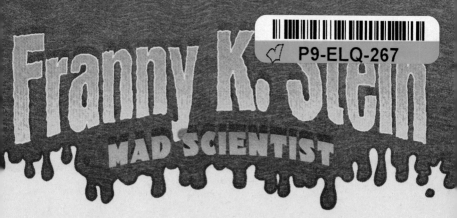

THE FRAN THAT TIME FORGOT

READ ALL OF FRANNY'S ADVENTURES

Lunch Walks Among Us
Attack of the 50-Ft. Cupid
The Invisible Fran
The Fran That Time Forgot

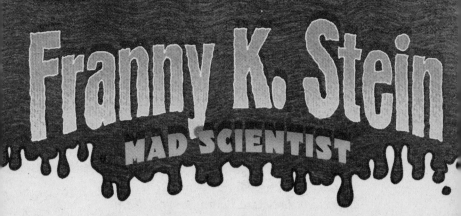

Franny K. Stein
MAD SCIENTIST

THE FRAN THAT TIME FORGOT

JIM BENTON

ALADDIN PAPERBACKS

NEW YORK   LONDON   TORONTO   SYDNEY

ACKNOWLEDGMENTS

Executive Editor: Kevin Lewis
Art Director: Dan Potash
Managing Editor: Dorothy Gribbin
Designer: Lucy Ruth Cummins
Production Manager: Chava Wolin
Editorial Assistant: Joanna Feliz
Paperback Assistant Editor: Molly McGuire

ALADDIN PAPERBACKS
An imprint of Simon & Schuster Children's Publishing Division
1230 Avenue of the Americas, New York, NY 10020
Copyright © 2005 by Jim Benton
All rights reserved, including the right of reproduction in whole or in part in any form.
ALADDIN PAPERBACKS and colophon are trademarks of Simon & Schuster, Inc.
Also available in a Simon & Schuster Books for Young Readers hardcover edition.
Designed by Dan Potash and Lucy Ruth Cummins
The text of this book was set in Captain Kidd.
Manufactured in the United States of America
First Aladdin Paperbacks edition October 2005
24 26 28 30 29 27 25
The Library of Congress has cataloged the hardcover edition as follows:
Benton, Jim. The Fran that time forgot / written and illustrated by Jim Benton.—1st ed.
p. cm.—(Franny K. Stein, mad scientist ; #4)
Summary: When her embarrassing middle name is revealed at school, mad scientist Franny K.
Stein experiments with time in order to return to the past and give herself a more dignified name.
ISBN-13: 978-0-689-86294-6 (hc.) ISBN-10: 0-689-86294-6 (hc.)
1. Science—Experiments—Fiction. 2. Time travel—Fiction.
3. Names, Personal—Fiction. 4. Humorous stories. I. Title.
PZ7.B447S47Fr 2005
[Fic]—dc22
2004011638
ISBN-13: 978-0-689-86298-4 (Aladdin pbk.) ISBN-10: 0-689-86298-9 (Aladdin pbk.)
1015 OFF

For
Griffin, Summer, Mary K,
Dan, Barb, Bruce, Mom, and Dad

CONTENTS

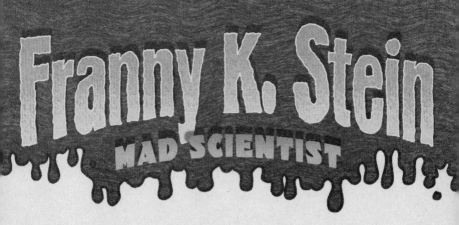

THE FRAN THAT TIME FORGOT

CHAPTER ONE
FRANNY'S HOUSE

The Stein family lived in the pretty pink house with lovely purple shutters down at the end of Daffodil Street. Everything about the house was bright and cheery. Everything, that is, except the upstairs bedroom with the tiny round window.

That tiny round window looked in on the bedroom and laboratory of Franny K. Stein, Little Girl Mad Scientist.

Recently, in this very lab, Franny had created Zero Gravity Dog Food, to make walking her dog, Igor, more fun.

And before that, she had invented Cannibalistic Broccoli that ate itself, so kids who hated eating vegetables would never have to.

And she still had a giant, hamster-powered trike, which she had created when she was only three years old.

She had been a mad scientist since she was just a baby. And Franny had been building and accumulating her creations in this lab as long as she could remember.

And she was very, very serious about it. She
always had been.

CHAPTER TWO

FRANNY'S FAMILY

The rest of Franny's family was not really interested in mad science.

Franny's dad was a regular dad. He loved
Franny, but he didn't really appreciate her
Voice-Activated Cheese Cannon, which provided
the user with an endless supply of cheeseballs
on demand. It just wasn't the sort of thing that
regular dads appreciated.

And Franny's mom was a regular mom. She loved Franny, but she didn't really appreciate things like the special chicken that Franny had bred with so many wishbones that you could wish for anything you wanted.

And Franny's little brother, Freddy, was a regular little brother. He loved Franny too (of course, he'd never admit it).

Freddy didn't appreciate her creations either. Especially when he found them under his bed at night.

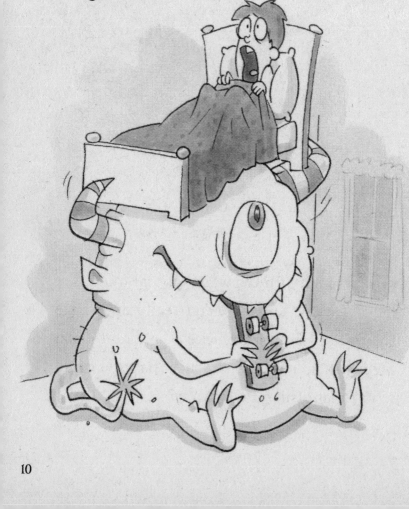

But even though they didn't always appreciate her creations, they had learned to take them seriously. When they didn't, it made Franny pretty angry, and the only thing more dangerous than a mad scientist is an angry mad scientist.

CHAPTER THREE

FRANNY TAKES THE CAKE

The announcement of the yearly Science Fair at school always filled Franny with mixed emotions. On the one hand, Franny loved creating new inventions and sharing them with others.

57. CREATE TALKING EGG SALAD

58. TURN BROTHER INTO PILE OF DIAPERS

59. BUILD MACHINE THAT CAN TRAVEL THROUGH TAPIOCA

60. MAKE A BAT-POWERED HELICOPTER

61. GROW SECOND HEAD

62. INVENT DEVICE THAT CHANGES BLACK JELLY BEANS INTO RED ONES.

63. CREATE ODOR THAT MAKES SKUNKS SICK

64. MAKE EVERYTHING MORE SCARY

65. TURN OCEANS TO COLA

66. MAKE

67. ...

On the other hand, Franny already had a long list of projects in her lab that she was anxious to complete.

And on the other hand, it was always an extra challenge to create a project that the kids at school would appreciate. Wait a second, that was *three* hands.

Well, this is Franny we're talking about.

Franny explained it to her mom. "I want to do a good Science Fair project, but I really don't like to take time away from the other lab projects."

Her mom smiled. "You can't have it both ways, Franny. You know what they say: You can't have your cake and eat it too."

A wide grin came across Franny's face. "You can't have your cake and eat it too? We'll see about that."

Franny walked quickly to her lab, with the blueprint of her next creation beginning to form inside her head as she went.

CHAPTER FOUR

IT WAS A PIECE OF CAKE

Franny began assembling the mechanism she had designed. "Can't have your cake and eat it too," she scoffed. "Where do they come up with these things?"

As she worked, Franny recalled when she conducted experiments based on other sayings she had heard her mom use.

AN APPLE A DAY KEEPS THE DOCTOR AWAY.
But it has to Be a REALLY BIG APPLE.

A BIRD IN THE HAND IS WORTH TWO IN THE BUSH.
BUT ARE YOU SURE YOU WANT A BIRD IN YOUR HAND?

WHOEVER SAID "AS EASY AS TAKING CANDY FROM A BABY"
NEVER ACTUALLY TRIED TO DO IT.

At last her device was complete, and she demonstrated it to her faithful assistant, Igor.

"Observe. Here, on my Time Warp Dessert Plate, I have a delicious piece of cake." Igor nodded. He was always ready to observe a delicious piece of cake.

Franny gobbled it up quickly. "Now I've eaten it. So, of course, I no longer have it."

Igor shook his head. No cake. That IS sad.

"But through a slight time warp, I can actually make a small zone on the plate go back to a point in the recent past when I had not yet eaten the cake."

Igor's eyes widened as the cake reappeared on Franny's special plate.

"And now I have it again," she said.

There was a way to have your cake and eat
it too, and Franny had figured it out.
"Easy as pie," she said.

CHAPTER FIVE
FROM FAIR TO CLOUDY

Miss Shelly smiled as the principal of the school, Mrs. Pierce, addressed all of the students. "Thank you all so much for working so hard to make this year's Science Fair exciting and interesting and not, uh, life threatening," she said.

The other kids knew exactly what Mrs. Pierce was talking about. In years past, some of Franny's creations had been a bit dangerous.

REMOTE CONTROL SCISSORS

PORCUPINE UNDERPANTS

SUGAR FROSTED SNAKES

TORNADO IN A JAR

CHICKEN FINGERS

25

In fact, most of Franny's creations could be
dangerous, and the kids had learned to be
very, very careful around anything that came
out of Franny's laboratory. They liked
Franny, but they had learned to take Franny
and her creations very seriously.

"We had many excellent entries, and this year we're giving out certificates," the principal said.

"I'm happy to present third prize to William Frederick Davis for his new breed of banana that you just turn inside out instead of peeling."

William smiled and ran up and took his certificate.

"I never knew his middle name was *Frederick*," Franny whispered, and suddenly she looked a bit concerned.

"Second prize goes to Anthony Christopher Hernandez for his Never-Miss Baseball Glove." Anthony ran up and got his certificate.

"*Christopher*, huh?" Franny said, looking slightly more concerned.

"And first prize," the principal began, "again goes to Franny—"

"Uh, that's okay," Franny interrupted nervously. "I'll, uh, just pass on the certificate."

"Of course not," Mrs. Pierce said. "You won fair and square, Franny. You should be proud."

"Okay, but you don't have to read my name or anything. We all know my name."

"Nonsense," the principal said. "For her Time Warp Dessert Plate, first prize goes to Franny *Kissypie* Stein."

CHAPTER SIX
WHAT'S IN A NAME

Franny *Kissypie* Stein. The principal looked at the certificate more closely just to make sure she had read it correctly. She even cleaned her glasses.

"Is that right, Franny? Is your middle name 'Kissypie'?"

SCIENCE FAIR AWARD

Franny
Kissypie
Stein

TIME WARP
DESSERT PLATE

1ST
Prize

Franny walked up and quietly took the certificate.

"Yes," Franny said. "It is. My middle name is Kissypie."

The kids looked at the principal. They looked at Miss Shelly. They looked at Franny. They looked at each other.

And then they erupted into an explosion of laughter. Franny *Kissypie* Stein. They could hardly believe it.

  "It's the most ridiculous name I ever heard!"
one of the kids shouted.

  "What kind of a middle name is that?"

  "We've been afraid of a kid named Kissypie?"

Even Miss Shelly and the principal giggled
a little. And Franny felt a terrible destructive
rage start to boil inside her.

"Silence!" Franny yelled, and her eyes flashed with her terrible, mad scientist anger.

"You think I want Kissypie for a middle name? It was some stupid nickname my dad had for my mom when they were just dating. They thought it would be cute to give it to me. I never asked to be named Kissypie."

Franny's face reddened and she spoke through clenched teeth. "Just in case none of you know how it works, your *parents* name you. You don't name yourself. Don't you think I'd change it if I had a way?"

"I bet you would," one of the kids yelled, and they all started laughing even harder.

Franny was so angry that she started to
tremble. She couldn't stand being laughed at.
She was just about to do something truly
awful when her eyes fell on her Time Warp
Dessert Plate.

Franny whispered to herself. "Don't you think I'd change it if I had a way?" Her mind began the calculations. "I wonder ..."

CHAPTER SEVEN

IT'S ONLY A MATTER OF TIME

Franny's mom watched as Franny carried calendars, watches, and hourglasses into her room. "More junk, Franny?" she said.

"I need this stuff, Mom. It's critical that I thoroughly understand the nature of time if this experiment is going to succeed."

"I know your experiments are important, Franny. But look at this room: bones everywhere, drawers full of guts. I suppose that banana peel is going to stay on the floor forever. Honestly, Franny, this is the sort of thing that attracts mice."

"I promise to clean it up, okay, Mom? But right now I have to finish this."

Franny's mom threw her arms into the air
and walked out, leaving Franny and Igor to the
experiment at hand.

CHAPTER EIGHT

I WONDER WHAT YESTERDAY WILL BE LIKE

It's really not much more complicated than the dessert plate, Igor. It just needs to work on me, instead of the cake, and I just have to travel *farther* into the past."

Franny showed Igor a copy of her birth certificate. "Here's what I need to change. See where it says 'Kissypie'? I'm going back in time and changing it to something more dignified— something people won't laugh at."

POP!

She strapped her Time Warper Device to her arm. "Wish me luck," Franny said, and she pressed a button. There was a flash, a pop, and a little puff of smoke, and she was gone.

Igor was scared. He had no idea where Franny was or, more frighteningly, *when* she was.

CHAPTER NINE
DOWN
MEMORY LANE

Franny hurtled back through time. She saw the time she faced a two-headed robot, a giant Cupid, and a Pumpkin-Crab Monster.

She saw the day she got Igor, the day she met Miss Shelly, and the day she first brought one of her teddy bears to life.

"I'm getting close," Franny said, and got
ready to press the STOP button on the Time
Warper.

She saw a familiar-looking baby girl in a
bassinet in a hospital nursery.

"This is it," Franny said, and she pressed the
button.

CHAPTER TEN

MAKING A NAME
FOR YOURSELF

There was a flash, and a pop, and a little puff of smoke, and Franny stood there, directly in front of Baby Franny.

Baby Franny blinked in astonishment as Franny grabbed Baby Franny's chart.

"I'm doing you a huge favor," she said to Baby Franny. "I'm changing this dumb middle name so that nobody can ever make fun of it again."

Franny erased "Kissypie." "Let's see," she said. "I still want to keep the initial *K.* How about 'Kidney'? Do you like the sound of that?"

Baby Franny scrunched up her nose.

"No, huh?" Franny said. "Maybe 'Khufu,' or 'Kismet,' or 'Kilowatt'?

Baby Franny pulled the pacifier from her mouth. "Kaboom," she said.

Franny smiled. "It's a bit peculiar, but I like it. It's like an explosion," she said, and she wrote "Kaboom" down as her middle name. Then she leaned way down and said, very seriously, to Baby Franny, "The most important thing is that nobody will laugh at us again. *There is nothing worse than being laughed at.*"

She picked up Baby Franny's toy elephant. "Here, let me fix that for you," she said, and drew a few extra eyes on it.

With a flash, and a pop, and a little puff of smoke, Franny was gone.

Baby Franny looked at the elephant with the extra eyes and smiled. At that moment she knew she wanted to create more things like that doll. At that moment, Baby Franny became a mad scientist.

CHAPTER ELEVEN

THERE'S NO TIME LIKE THE PRESENT

Franny started hurtling forward again in time, back to the present. "I was kind of cute when I was a baby," she said, smiling.

"I wonder how I'll look when I'm older," she said, tapping her finger on her chin. (Franny was a very curious girl.)

"Since I have the Time Warper Device running, I guess it wouldn't hurt to have a little peek into the future," she said, and she went right past the present and into the future.

With a flash, and a pop, and a little puff of smoke, Franny found herself in front of her house, sometime in the future.

CHAPTER TWELVE

YOU SHOULD BE ASHAMED OF YOURSELF

At least, Franny thought this was her house. Thick smoke poured out of a huge chimney that punched out through the roof. Rusty drums of chemicals lay all over the yard. Terrible howls and screeches came from unseen creatures hiding within.

"I like what they've done with the place,"
Franny said approvingly. "I'm just surprised
that Mom decided to go with this look. She's
usually so fussy."

Franny eased her way past the front door, which was hanging by a single hinge. Inside, the living room was crawling with snakes and spiders and things that looked like maybe they were half snake and half spider. "Perhaps a bit much," Franny said. "Still, it's quite cozy."

There was no sign of her family anywhere. Even Igor, who would have run to the door to meet her, was gone.

She tiptoed up the stairs toward her bedroom laboratory and quietly pushed the door
open.

There, feverishly banging on a fiendish-looking device, was a tall mad scientist that Franny knew could only be herself as a teenager.

CHAPTER THIRTEEN
WILL YOU JUST LISTEN TO YOURSELF?

Teen Franny twisted the final screw on the machine she was constructing. "The Monster Multiplier is finally complete. They were foolish to laugh at me," she grumbled as she began throwing switches. The Monster Multiplier started to whine and sizzle.

"But no more. Let's see how they like it when these monsters begin overrunning the planet. Soon they'll take over the entire world. There'll be no laughing then."

The Monster Multiplier crackled. The door opened and out walked a monster. It looked a lot like the elephant toy she had decorated for Baby Franny, but a lot bigger.

It crackled again, and again the door opened. An identical elephant-monster walked out.

Soon the machine was making monster after monster. They jumped out the window and began waging terror on the streets. "It won't be long now," Teen Franny said, and she grinned a mad scientist smile—an evil mad scientist smile. "It won't be long before all the laughing stops."

Franny gasped. Teen Franny was pretty handy in the monster-making machine department, and you had to give her credit for that. But she was evil. She was way beyond an acceptable amount of evil. She was really and truly evil—the kind of evil that had to be stopped.

"I did this to myself," Franny said. "I never should have gone back in time, and I never should have changed my middle name."

And she never should have walked backward into the arms of a five-eyed elephant-monster, but she did that, too.

CHAPTER FOURTEEN

YOU SHOULD HAVE GOTTEN A GRIP ON YOURSELF BEFORE YOURSELF GOT A GRIP ON YOU

Teen Franny looked angrily at Franny, who was struggling to free herself from the arms of the five-eyed monster. "So what was it?" Teen Franny said. "Some sort of a time machine? Sounds like something I might do."

"That's exactly what I did," Franny said.
"It's a beautiful, classic piece of mad science."

Teen Franny huffed and pushed one of her monsters out the window.

"Please," Franny said. "You have to stop this. I mean—don't get me wrong—I'm a huge fan of monsters, and I'm even fond of an occasional rampage. But what you're planning is beyond that. This is not just mad science. This is evil mad science. Why are you doing this?"

Teen Franny's eyes narrowed. "C'mon, Franny. You're me. You know why."

Franny shook her head. "Really, I don't."

Teen Franny cruelly flicked a spider with her finger. "The Science Fair, Franny. Remember the Science Fair?"

CHAPTER FIFTEEN

IS THERE AN ECHO IN HERE? IS THERE AN ECHO IN HERE?

I'll bet this is because I made my middle name too extreme," Franny whispered. "The name Kaboom is like an explosion. *This* version of me grew up with a name that sounded like utter destruction."

Teen Franny rummaged through a trunk. "Here it is," she said, and she showed it to Franny. Behind some cracked glass was the certificate from the Science Fair made out to Franny Kaboom Stein.

Teen Franny turned up her Monster Multiplier, and the monsters started popping out faster and faster.

"You asked me why I'm doing this, kid. It was because they laughed. They laughed at my middle name, and they laughed at me."

Franny thought, *Wait a second. They laughed at the name "Kissypie," but I had no idea that they would laugh at the name "Kaboom." They would have laughed at "Kismet" or "Khufu" or "Kidney." This had nothing to do with the name.*

Teen Franny spoke through clenched teeth. "The most important thing is that nobody will laugh at us again. *There is nothing worse than being laughed at.*"

Those were Franny's precise words coming back to haunt her. That was exactly what she had told herself as a baby.

Suddenly Franny understood that none of this was about changing her name to Kaboom. This was all because of what she had said to Baby Franny about laughing.

Teen Franny looked out the window as her monsters began tearing the neighbors' homes to pieces, and she smiled an evil smile.

Franny said to herself, "Think! Think! Think!"

CHAPTER SIXTEEN

ONE MORE REASON TO NEVER CLEAN YOUR ROOM

Franny couldn't get away, and she couldn't reach the controls on her Time Warper Device.

Suddenly a thought occurred to her.

Franny looked around and spotted her old Voice-Activated Cheese Cannon. "Cheddar!" she shouted, and caught the cannonball of cheese it launched her way.

VOOM!

Teen Franny spun around. "Hold it right there, kid," she said. "I know what you're thinking. You're thinking that cheese will attract the mice, and then the mice will scare the elephant-monster, which will drop you, and then you'll escape. Am I right?"

Franny said nothing.

"Of course I'm right," Teen Franny sneered. "I'm just as clever as you are, Franny. But two principles in your dumb little plan are entirely incorrect: Mice don't *really* like cheese, and elephants aren't *really* afraid of mice."

"I guess you're right," Franny said. "But *my* plan was based on the principle that nobody likes it when you stuff wads of cheese up their nose," she said as she did exactly that. "*And* I never, ever, ever cleaned up my room."

The elephant-monster, struggling to dislodge the cheese wad from its trunk, took two steps backward and slipped on the banana peel that had been in that exact spot for years, just as Franny's mom had predicted. As the monster fell, it released Franny.

SHLORP!

Teen Franny lunged for one of the countless inventions lying around the lab. She aimed the Frog-O-Matic and fired it at Franny. Franny swiftly grabbed a mirror and deflected the ray.

Teen Franny picked up the electric Molecule Destroyer and switched it on. Franny quickly unplugged it from the wall.

"This is my lab too, you know," Franny said. "I made most of this junk. I know how it works," and she fired a Freeze Ray at Teen Franny.

Teen Franny fired a Heat Ray back and the rays cancelled each other out.

"Yeah," Teen Franny said. "I know how it all works too. And while we stand here battling, my elephant-monsters continue to multiply. And besides, you bratty little kid, we may be the same person, but I'm the older version. That means I know everything you know, plus a little bit more. You can't defeat me."

Franny knew that Teen Franny was right. She closed her eyes and thought as hard as she could.

Suddenly an idea came to her.

POP!

"Oh, yes I can," Franny said, and she pushed
a button on the Time Warper Device. With a
flash, and a pop, and a little puff of smoke, she
was gone.

CHAPTER SEVENTEEN

HE WHO LAUGHS FIRST, LAUGHS LAST

Franny was suddenly back at the Science Fair. Anthony Christopher Hernandez had just gotten his certificate for his Never-Miss Baseball Glove, and Franny looked very concerned, again.

"And first prize," the principal began, "again goes to Franny—"

"Uh, that's okay," Franny interrupted nervously. "I'll, uh, just pass on the certificate."

"Of course not," Mrs. Pierce said. "You won fair and square, Franny. You should be proud."

"Okay, but you don't have to read my name or anything. We all know my name."

"Nonsense," the principal said. "For her Time Warp Dessert Plate, first prize goes to Franny *Kaboom* Stein."

The principal looked at the certificate more closely just to make sure she had read it correctly. She even cleaned her glasses.

"Is that right, Franny? Is your middle name 'Kaboom'?"

Franny walked up and quietly took the certificate.

"Yes," Franny said. "It is. My middle name is Kaboom."

The kids looked at the principal. They looked at Miss Shelly. They looked at Franny. They looked at each other.

And then they erupted into an explosion of laughter. Franny *Kaboom* Stein. They could hardly believe it.

"It's the most ridiculous name I ever heard!" one of the kids shouted.

"What kind of a middle name is that?"

Even Miss Shelly and the principal giggled a little. And Franny felt a terrible destructive rage start to boil inside her.

Franny knew she had one chance to beat Teen Franny and the horrible future that awaited her if she did not.

I didn't have to change my name, she thought. *I had to change how I felt about people laughing at it.*

And Franny smiled.

And then she chuckled. And she laughed. "Kaboom," she said. "You're right, it is a pretty ridiculous name." And Franny suddenly didn't really mind the kids laughing. It was a silly name, and it made her laugh too.

There are a lot of things worse than being laughed at, she thought.

CHAPTER EIGHTEEN

A FUTURE WITH APPEAL

The next day Franny cleaned up the lab just like she had promised her mom. They cleaned up the drawers full of guts, organized the boxes of bones, and took Franny's first-place certificate out of the trunk and hung it proudly on the wall.

Franny even allowed herself another giggle at the name Kaboom. Laughing at yourself was much easier than she used to believe.

Franny's lab was still pretty cluttered, but it looked better than ever, and Franny knew, deep down, that she would never, ever, ever grow up into the evil Teen Franny she had seen on her journey into the future.

Of course, they left the banana peel right
where she might need it to be...

just in case.